This is a work of fiction. Similarities to real people, places, or events are entirely coincidental.

SHORT SCARY STORY FOR KIDS AGE 9-12

First edition. September 20, 2023.

Copyright © 2023 mahdi amini.

ISBN: 979-8223344698

Written by mahdi amini.

Table of Contents

short scary story for kids age 9-12

horror stories about monsters, ghost, witches and more to tell on campfire or where you want

Author Name: mahdi amini

The Enchanted Lantern

On a warm summer night, a group of kids aged 9-12 gathered around a crackling campfire deep in the heart of the woods. They were on a thrilling camping adventure, sharing laughter and marshmallow treats under the twinkling stars. As the fire's glow danced in their eyes, one of the older campers, Sarah, decided it was the perfect time to share a ghostly tale.

"Listen closely, everyone," Sarah said with a mischievous grin. "I have a chilling story to share with you all—the legend of the Enchanted Lantern."

The younger campers leaned in, their excitement growing as Sarah began her story.

"Long ago, there was a small village nestled among these very woods. It was said that every year, on the night of the full moon, a ghostly figure would appear, holding a mysterious lantern that glowed with an otherworldly light."

"The villagers were afraid, believing the figure to be a restless spirit searching for something it had lost in life. They called it 'The Wandering Light' and kept their distance, leaving the lantern undisturbed."

"But one brave young girl named Amelia was curious. She had heard the stories, and her heart swelled with compassion for the ghostly visitor. One moonlit night, she decided to follow the soft glow of the lantern into the depths of the forest."

"The woods were eerily silent as Amelia walked deeper into the darkness. The lantern's light seemed to lead her on an enchanted path, guiding her through the trees and under the moon's watchful gaze."

"As she ventured further, Amelia stumbled upon an ancient, overgrown graveyard. The Wandering Light floated gently over a forgotten grave, illuminating a name etched in a weathered tombstone."

"To Amelia's surprise, the ghostly figure turned and beckoned her closer. Brimming with courage, she stepped forward, and with each step, the lantern's glow grew stronger, revealing the spirit's sad, but gentle face."

"Amelia could feel the spirit's longing and sadness. Through her tears, the ghostly figure spoke in a soft, ethereal voice. 'Thank you for coming, young one. I am William, a lost soul bound to this realm by the magic of this lantern. I need your help to find peace.'"

"Amelia asked how she could assist William. He explained that his lantern had been stolen by a mischievous spirit, and without it, he couldn't cross over to the afterlife."

"Determined to help, Amelia promised to retrieve the stolen lantern. William's face brightened with hope, and he entrusted her with a small, glowing crystal that would guide her to the spirit's lair."

"Amelia followed the crystal's light to an ancient tree hollow where the mischievous spirit dwelled. With wit and kindness, she persuaded the spirit to return the lantern."

"Overjoyed, William took hold of his beloved lantern, and a radiant light enveloped him. With a grateful smile, he whispered his thanks to Amelia before ascending into the night sky, finally finding the peace he had sought for centuries."

"The village rejoiced when they learned of Amelia's brave deed, and every year, on the night of the full moon, they celebrated the Enchanted Lantern, remembering the young girl who had helped a lost soul find its way home."

As Sarah finished her story, the campers sat in awe, their hearts filled with wonder and a newfound appreciation for the magic that may reside in even the most unexpected places. From that night on, the legend of the Enchanted Lantern became a cherished tale among the campers, a story they would pass down to future generations, keeping the spirit of bravery and compassion alive under the moonlit skies.

The Whispering Woods

Once upon a time, in a small town surrounded by a dense forest, there was a group of adventurous kids spending their summer at a campsite. The campsite was famous for its spooky stories, and one tale, in particular, sent shivers down their spines the legend of the Whispering Woods.

As the sun dipped below the horizon, casting long shadows over the campfire, the kids huddled close, eager to hear the chilling tale. Their campfire guide, an old man named Mr. Jenkins, spoke with a mysterious twinkle in his eyes.

"Long ago," he began, "this forest was home to a group of friendly woodland creatures. They lived in harmony with nature until one fateful day, a greedy lumberjack arrived. He cared not for the balance of the forest and began cutting down trees, leaving destruction in his wake."

"The woodland creatures tried to reason with the lumberjack, but he ignored their pleas. The forest grew restless and, in its sorrow, conjured a ghostly presence known as 'The Whisperer.' This spirit, though invisible, carried a haunting voice that echoed through the woods."

Mr. Jenkins paused, letting the kids' imagination run wild. The crackling of the campfire seemed to mimic the eerie echoes of the Whisperer.

"The lumberjack continued to fell trees, blind to the warnings of the Whisperer. As night fell, he heard soft whispers calling his name, but he dismissed them as tricks of the wind. Unbeknownst to him, the Whisperer grew stronger, fueled by the forest's pain."

"One night, as the lumberjack slept in his tent, the Whisperer's voice grew louder, more insistent. It echoed through the woods like a mournful cry. The lumberjack awoke in a cold sweat, terror in his eyes. He realized he had angered the spirit of the forest."

"Filled with remorse, the lumberjack vowed to mend his ways. He planted new trees and treated the forest with respect. But the Whisperer's haunting whispers never ceased, a reminder of the forest's pain and the lumberjack's greed."

"Legend has it that even today, if you listen closely in these woods, you can hear the faint whispers of the Whisperer, urging everyone to protect and cherish nature."

The kids sat in awe, the shadows of the trees dancing around them. The campfire's glow added an enchanting touch to the tale.

"And so," Mr. Jenkins concluded, "remember this story when you venture into the woods. Respect the balance of nature, and you may never hear the whispers of the Whisperer."

As the campfire guide finished his story, the kids exchanged nervous glances, but their curiosity about the Whispering Woods lingered. They went to bed that night, their minds filled with both fear and wonder, dreaming of woodland creatures and ghostly whispers under the moonlit sky.

Little did they know that their campfire story had sparked a newfound appreciation for nature, leaving a lasting impression on their young hearts. From that night on, they promised to be guardians of the forest, ensuring that the legend of the Whispering Woods lived on for generations to come.

The Haunting at Moonstone Manor

In the heart of the countryside, nestled amidst towering trees and fog-covered hills, stood Moonstone Manor—an old, abandoned house that sent shivers down the spines of those who dared to pass by. Local legends whispered of a spooky ghost haunting the manor, leaving a trail of eerie tales in its wake.

One fateful autumn evening, a group of adventurous friends aged 9-12 decided to explore the rumored haunted house. Emma, Jake, Lily, and Ben had heard chilling stories about the ghost that roamed the corridors of Moonstone Manor. Undeterred, they armed themselves with flashlights and a sense of excitement.

As they approached the manor, a cold wind whispered through the overgrown garden, rustling the leaves and adding to the eerie ambiance. The moon hid behind a blanket of clouds, casting an ominous glow on the decrepit mansion.

With trembling hands and racing hearts, the kids pushed open the creaky front door. The inside was shrouded in darkness, except for the faint light of their flashlights. A feeling of unease settled upon them, but their curiosity pushed them forward.

The friends explored room after room, each filled with remnants of the past—dusty furniture, old paintings, and forgotten toys. As they climbed the creaking stairs to the upper floors, the atmosphere grew heavier, and their flashlights flickered as if battling against an unseen force.

In the dim light, Emma thought she saw a shadowy figure out of the corner of her eye. Her heart skipped a beat, and she whispered to the others, "Did you see that?"

Nervous glances were exchanged, but they continued onward. They reached the attic, the air thick with mystery. Suddenly, a chilling voice echoed through the darkness, causing their hearts to race.

"Get out! Leave this place!" the voice rasped, sending shivers down their spines.

Fearful but resolute, they called out, "Who are you? Why are you haunting this house?"

The ghostly figure materialized before them—an ethereal, transparent figure with glowing eyes. It seemed to be both sad and angry.

"I am the spirit of Abigail, a young girl who once lived in this house," the ghost spoke with a haunting echo. "I cannot rest, for a dark secret binds me to this place."

Curiosity mixed with compassion in the hearts of the young explorers. "What secret?" they asked in unison.

Abigail recounted a tragic tale of betrayal and treachery that had taken place within Moonstone Manor many years ago. The truth had been buried with her, and her soul was trapped in the house until someone could help her find peace.

Determined to help the restless spirit, the friends promised to uncover the truth and bring closure to Abigail's spirit. They researched old archives, interviewed townspeople, and pieced together the events of the past.

In the end, they discovered the hidden truth—a deceitful relative had wronged Abigail, leading to her untimely demise. Armed with the evidence, the kids returned to the manor to confront the ghost.

With tears streaming down her translucent cheeks, Abigail finally found solace as they revealed the truth. A bright light enveloped her, and she vanished, leaving behind an aura of peace.

From that night on, Moonstone Manor was no longer haunted by the spooky ghost. The legend of Abigail's haunting became a tale of bravery and compassion shared among the children, and the old house stood as a reminder of their courageous adventure, forever etched in their hearts.

The Ghost of Whispering Pines

Around a crackling campfire in the heart of Whispering Pines Campground, a group of kids aged 9-12 gathered for a night of spooky stories. The fire's glow danced in their eyes, casting eerie shadows on the surrounding trees. Among the campers was an older boy named Alex, known for his chilling tales. Tonight, he had a special ghost story to share.

"Listen up, everyone," Alex said, his voice low and mysterious. "Tonight, I'll tell you the haunting tale of the Ghost of Whispering Pines."

The younger campers leaned in closer, eager to be spooked.

"Many years ago," Alex began, "there was a young girl named Emily who loved the Whispering Pines Campground. She visited every summer with her family, reveling in the joy of nature and the campfire tales told under these very stars."

"One summer, while exploring the woods, Emily stumbled upon an old, weathered cabin hidden deep in the heart of the forest. Intrigued, she ventured inside and discovered a beautiful music box. When she opened it, a hauntingly beautiful melody filled the air."

"The music box belonged to a ghostly figure—a young girl named Lily—who had once lived in the cabin. She had been a camper at Whispering Pines many years before Emily was born."

"As the legend goes, Lily's life was cut short tragically when a fierce storm struck the campground. Lost and alone, her spirit remained trapped in the cabin, longing for someone to share her story with."

"Emily, brave and compassionate, decided to help Lily find peace. Each night, they met by the campfire, and Emily would listen to Lily's tales of the past, her laughter and tears woven into the melody of the music box."

"But as the days passed, Emily noticed that something was amiss. The beautiful music had taken a darker, haunting tone. Lily's spirit seemed troubled, and strange occurrences began to haunt the campground."

"Whispers filled the night air, and campers reported feeling an icy presence on their shoulders. Footsteps echoed in the distance, but no one could be seen."

"Emily knew she had to uncover the truth behind Lily's unrest. She delved into the campground's history and discovered a long-forgotten secret—a promise that had been broken many years ago."

"Determined to set things right, Emily followed Lily's guidance and returned to the cabin. With a heart full of courage, she honored the forgotten promise, and a soft, radiant light enveloped Lily's spirit."

"In that moment, the music box's melody turned pure and sweet once more, and Lily's spirit finally found peace. Her ghostly figure vanished, leaving behind a faint whisper of gratitude in the wind."

"From that night on, Whispering Pines Campground held a new enchantment. Emily's bravery and compassion had not only put a ghost to rest but had also filled the woods with a sense of wonder and magic."

As Alex finished his tale, the campers looked around the whispering pines, their imaginations running wild. The campfire's warmth and the story's eerie atmosphere left them with a mix of excitement and trepidation. But they knew that the Ghost of Whispering Pines would forever be a part of the camp's history—a tale of bravery, friendship, and the magical encounters that could happen under the watchful eyes of the stars.

Spectral Guardians of the Dark Forest

In the heart of a dense and ominous forest, where moonlight struggled to penetrate the thick canopy, there was a legend whispered among the locals about ghostly protectors that roamed the shadows—the Spectral Guardians. These ethereal beings were said to be the spirits of ancient warriors who had fallen defending the forest from harm.

Deep within the dark forest, a group of brave kids aged 9-12, comprising Sofia, Lucas, and Maya, embarked on a thrilling adventure. They were determined to uncover the truth behind the legend of the Spectral Guardians and the wolves said to roam the forest alongside them.

One moonlit night, as they huddled around a campfire, the chilling howls of wolves echoed through the woods, raising goosebumps on their skin. Undeterred, they shared stories of courage and bravery, unknowingly calling upon the attention of the Spectral Guardians.

Suddenly, amidst the flickering flames, a spectral figure materialized before them. Translucent and awe-inspiring, the Guardian's eyes glowed like orbs of ancient wisdom. The children gasped, their hearts pounding with a mix of fear and fascination.

"I am Orel, one of the Spectral Guardians," the ethereal figure spoke with a voice that echoed like a whisper carried on the wind. "The forest's balance is threatened, and the wolves you hear are not what they seem."

Sofia, the bravest of the trio, gathered her courage and asked, "What do you mean, Orel? Are the wolves dangerous?"

Orel nodded solemnly. "Not all of them, but a dark force has corrupted some of the wolves, turning them into malevolent spirits that seek to harm the forest's delicate ecosystem."

Lucas, always curious, inquired, "How can we help, Orel?"

The Guardian smiled faintly. "Only those with pure hearts and the will to protect the forest can aid us. You must venture deeper into the heart of the forest and find the ancient wellspring—the source of the forest's life force."

Maya, the empathetic one, nodded. "We promise to protect the forest and restore its balance. Please guide us, Orel." Encouraged by the children's determination, Orel bestowed them with ancient amulets that glowed with a gentle light. These amulets would shield them from harm and connect them with the essence of the forest. With their amulets protecting them, the kids ventured deeper into the forest, their footsteps muffled by the thick carpet of fallen leaves. The wolves' haunting howls guided their path.

As they reached the ancient wellspring, they encountered the corrupted wolves, eyes glowing with malevolence. But the amulets' magic shielded them from harm, and they sensed the sorrow hidden within the wolves' malicious intent.

Drawing upon the compassion in their hearts, they revealed the truth to the corrupted wolves—the forest's life force was fading, and their malevolence was only hastening its demise.

The wolves, touched by the children's words, relinquished their malevolent ways, and their eyes lost their sinister glow. Instead, they embraced their true role as guardians of the forest. In that moment, the amulets glowed brighter, and the Spectral Guardians appeared once more, a shimmering array of benevolent spirits.

"You have done well, young ones," Orel commended. "The forest's balance is restored, and the wolves will now protect and preserve its harmony."

From that night on, the legend of the Spectral Guardians and the wolves of the dark forest was rewritten—a tale of courage, compassion, and the profound connection between humanity and nature. And the children, forever changed by their encounter, continued to cherish and protect the forest they now knew was watched over by its spectral protectors.

Whispers of the Malevolent Shadows

In the heart of a desolate town, where the chilling wind swept through dark, abandoned alleyways, a sinister presence lurked. The locals spoke in hushed whispers of the malevolent shadows that haunted the streets at night, spreading an aura of horror that sent shivers down even the bravest souls.

One gloomy evening, a group of curious teenagers ventured into the town's forbidden territory. Sarah, Mark, and Alex were thrill-seekers, drawn by the allure of the unknown. They entered a decaying, derelict mansion, where the wind howled through broken windows, creating haunting melodies that echoed through the halls.

As darkness enveloped them, the air grew heavy with a palpable sense of dread. The faint moonlight cast eerie shadows on the walls, twisting the once-familiar surroundings into a labyrinth of terror.

The friends explored the mansion, their flashlights piercing the darkness. Every creak of the floorboards and every rustle of the wind seemed like a malevolent whisper from the unknown.

Suddenly, Mark's flashlight flickered and died, leaving them in pitch darkness. Panic seized their hearts as they tried to find their way out, but the oppressive shadows seemed to close in around them.

A chilling laughter echoed through the halls, causing their blood to run cold. It seemed as if the darkness itself had come to life, mocking their intrusion into its domain.

Amidst the horror, Alex managed to ignite a small candle he had brought with him. Its feeble flame fought against the oppressive shadows, offering a glimmer of hope in the darkness.

As the wind howled outside, they heard something else—a sinister whisper that seemed to emanate from the very walls of the mansion. Dread consumed them, but they knew they had to press on if they wanted to escape the clutches of this malevolence.

They found themselves in a grand ballroom, its once-elegant decor now shrouded in decay. The wind's mournful wailing grew louder, and the shadows seemed to dance around them, twisting and contorting in unnatural ways.

In the flickering candlelight, they spotted an old diary left on a dusty piano. Sarah cautiously opened it and read aloud the harrowing tale of a vengeful spirit who had once lived in the mansion. It spoke of betrayal, heartbreak, and a curse that bound the spirit to the darkness for eternity.

The candle's flame wavered, threatening to extinguish, but the teens were determined to end the curse and escape the horror that surrounded them.

With trembling hands, they formed a circle, clasping each other tightly. Together, they chanted a mantra of courage and unity, breaking the curse that bound the vengeful spirit to the mansion.

A blinding light filled the ballroom as the malevolent shadows retreated. The wind outside turned into a gentle breeze, carrying away the echoes of the past.

When the light subsided, the mansion was no longer a place of horror. Instead, it stood as a reminder of the courage and camaraderie that had banished the darkness within.

As they stepped outside, the first rays of dawn painted the sky with hues of pink and gold. The town, once shrouded in darkness, now glimmered with the promise of a new day.

From that night on, the legend of the brave teenagers who confronted the shadows and dispelled the horror became a tale of resilience and friendship, whispered through generations as a reminder that even in the darkest of times, the light of hope and unity can prevail.

The Tale of the Monsters' Friends

In a world where shadows stretched long and the night held its breath, there existed a realm shrouded in mystery and darkness. This realm was known as the Enchanted Abyss, a place where monsters of unimaginable shapes and sizes lurked in the deepest corners, waiting to emerge under the moon's eerie glow.

In a quaint village, nestled on the outskirts of the Enchanted Abyss, lived a group of intrepid children aged 9-12—Sam, Emma, and Jake. Curiosity and bravery coursed through their veins, and tales of the monstrous creatures in the Abyss only fueled their desire for adventure.

One moonlit night, as the village slept, the trio embarked on a daring expedition to the Abyss. Armed with courage and a secret map passed down through generations, they crept through the forest, guided by the ghostly glow of fireflies.

As they approached the Abyss, the air grew heavy with anticipation. The forest's rustling leaves seemed to whisper cautionary tales of the monsters that lay ahead.

With trepidation and excitement, they crossed the threshold into the Enchanted Abyss. An otherworldly aura surrounded them as they ventured deeper into the darkness.

Their hearts pounded as they encountered their first monster—a towering, shadowy figure with fiery eyes and gnarled claws. Sam, with a voice that quivered but didn't falter, addressed the creature.

"Who are you?" he asked bravely, determined to understand the enigmatic beings that inhabited the Abyss.

To their surprise, the monster spoke in a rumbling, mournful tone. "I am Grom, the Guardian of Lost Dreams. I once roamed the land above, but I was banished here for failing to protect the dreams of a young girl."

The children listened intently as Grom shared his tale of remorse and redemption. Empathy washed over them, and they promised to help him find the young girl's dreams and restore her happiness.

As they delved further into the Abyss, they encountered more monsters, each with their own unique stories—monsters of sorrow, laughter, and forgotten memories. Some were misunderstood, others simply lost.

With open hearts and unwavering determination, the children forged connections with the monsters and helped heal the wounds that had bound them to the Enchanted Abyss.

As the sun began to rise on the horizon, casting its warm embrace on the Abyss, the children stood amidst a gathering of grateful monsters. The once-menacing creatures had transformed into gentle beings, their eyes reflecting newfound hope.

A solemn cheer echoed through the Abyss as the children bid farewell to their newfound friends. They returned to their village, forever changed by their extraordinary encounter.

From that day on, the children became known as the "Monsters' Friends," and their tale of compassion and courage spread far and wide. The Enchanted Abyss was no longer feared, but rather admired for its inhabitants' resilience and the bond between monsters and humans.

And so, the Monsters' Friends continued to venture into the Enchanted Abyss, fostering friendships with creatures beyond imagination and proving that beneath even the most frightening exteriors, there lies the potential for understanding, compassion, and the magic of true friendship.

The Campfire Encounter

In the heart of a dense forest, a group of young campers had set up a campfire under the twinkling stars. Among them was a curious and adventurous girl named Lily, who loved to hear and share spooky stories. The night was alive with the crackling of the fire, and the forest seemed to come alive with mysterious sounds.

As the campers laughed and roasted marshmallows, Lily noticed a pair of glowing eyes peering at them from the shadows. Intrigued, she motioned to her friends, and they all turned their attention to the source of the mysterious gaze.

To their surprise, a large figure emerged from the darkness—it was a bear, standing tall on its hind legs. A gasp escaped the campers as they thought it might be a monster, but Lily recognized it as a friendly black bear she had seen in the woods before.

With a mix of fear and fascination, they watched as the bear approached their campfire. It seemed unafraid and almost curious about their presence.

"Is it a monster?" one of the campers whispered.

Lily shook her head, her voice steady as she said, "No, it's a bear. They're not monsters; they're creatures of the forest, just like us."

As if understanding her words, the bear settled down near the campfire, its eyes never leaving the group. Lily felt a strange connection with the majestic creature and decided to offer it a marshmallow as a gesture of friendship.

To her surprise, the bear gently took the marshmallow from her hand and seemed to enjoy it. The other campers watched in amazement as Lily continued to share treats with the bear. As the night wore on, Lily and her friends realized that the bear wasn't a fearsome monster but a gentle and curious being. They laughed and shared stories, all the while having an unexpected guest at their campfire. The bear, in turn, seemed to enjoy the company of these curious humans. Its eyes sparkled with warmth as if appreciating the bond that had formed.

Eventually, it was time to bid farewell to their newfound friend. Lily whispered her gratitude to the bear, and with a contented look, it retreated back into the shadows of the forest.

As the campers settled in for the night, Lily couldn't help but smile, knowing that her encounter with the "monster bear" had turned into an extraordinary and heartwarming experience. From that night on, the campfire story of Lily and the Friendly Monster Bear became a cherished memory among the campers, reminding them that sometimes, what might seem like a monster can be a magical friend in disguise. And as they returned to the same campsite each year, they would always look forward to the possibility of another enchanting encounter with their friendly forest companion.

The Enigmatic Clown

In a quiet town, where laughter once echoed through the streets, an eerie presence loomed—the mysterious disappearance of children. Each time a child vanished, rumors of a sinister clown haunting the shadows spread like wildfire.

Among the town's children, there was a brave and quick-witted girl named Mia. She had heard the chilling tales of the clown but refused to be consumed by fear. Determined to uncover the truth, she embarked on her own investigation, seeking clues that might lead to the missing children.

One moonlit night, as Mia sneaked through the deserted fairground, she stumbled upon a hidden passage beneath the old Ferris wheel. Intrigued, she followed it, her heart pounding with both fear and curiosity.

The passage led her to a hidden chamber where she found the missing children, sitting in a trance-like state, surrounded by eerie carnival decorations. At the center of the chamber stood the enigmatic clown, his face hidden behind a grotesque mask.

Suppressing her fear, Mia knew she had to act quickly. She bravely confronted the clown, demanding answers.

"Why have you taken the children?" she asked, her voice steady despite the terror that threatened to overwhelm her.

The clown's response was cryptic, speaking in riddles that only deepened the mystery. Mia's determination grew, and she realized that the clown was no supernatural entity but a person with malevolent intentions.

Realizing that the lives of the kidnapped children were in her hands, Mia hatched a daring plan. With her quick thinking and resourcefulness, she managed to outsmart the clown and release the children from their trance.

Together, they made a stealthy escape from the hidden chamber, careful not to alert the clown. As they emerged into the moonlit night, the fairground seemed to come alive with the rustling of leaves and the haunting calliope music.

Mia led the children through the maze-like paths, knowing that their safety depended on her bravery and determination.

With the dawn approaching, they finally reached the edge of the fairground. Mia made sure the children were safe before returning to confront the clown once more.

In a final showdown, Mia showed incredible bravery, facing the sinister clown head-on. As the first rays of sunlight pierced through the darkness, the clown's mask slipped off, revealing a desperate person seeking vengeance.

Empathy filled Mia's heart, realizing that the clown's actions were born out of a painful past. In an unexpected turn of events, she extended her hand in compassion, offering a chance for redemption and forgiveness.

With tears in their eyes, the clown accepted Mia's hand, releasing the grip of darkness that had consumed them.

As the town woke up to the return of their missing children, Mia's courageous actions became a beacon of hope and bravery. The tale of the Enigmatic Clown transformed from a chilling mystery to a story of compassion, forgiveness, and the power of one young girl's unwavering determination to save her friends and offer a second chance to those lost in the depths of darkness.

The Demon's Redemption: Rise of a Hero

In a world torn by darkness and chaos, a powerful demon named Azol had once wreaked havoc upon the realms. His malevolence had left a trail of devastation in its wake, and his name struck fear into the hearts of both mortals and immortals alike.

But deep within Azol's tormented soul, a glimmer of goodness remained—a spark of light that had been buried beneath the weight of his past. As he roamed the realms, he witnessed the suffering caused by his own actions and felt a pang of remorse.

One fateful day, Azol encountered a young child, defenseless and alone, trapped in the clutches of evil. The child's innocent eyes mirrored the darkness he once possessed, and in that moment, something changed within him.

Moved by the child's vulnerability, Azol found himself stepping forward, defying his own malevolence to protect the innocent soul. With a newfound purpose, he fought against the forces of darkness and rescued the child, vowing to be their protector. As the days passed, Azol's transformation continued. He discovered that helping others and defending the weak ignited a sense of purpose and fulfillment he had never known before.

News of the demon hero spread like wildfire, and those who had once feared him now looked to him as a symbol of hope and redemption.

But not all were convinced of Azol's change. Dark forces sought to exploit his inner conflict, tempting him to return to his malevolent ways. The constant battle against his own demons tested his resolve, but with each victory, he grew stronger.

The child he had rescued, now named Aria, became his steadfast companion—a beacon of innocence and purity that reminded him of the goodness he had long suppressed.

In the face of overwhelming darkness, Azol and Aria ventured to the heart of the realms, where the ultimate evil threatened to consume everything. They confronted the malevolent entity that had once corrupted Azol, facing the darkest parts of his past.

It was a battle of wills and inner demons a struggle to choose between darkness and light. As the forces of darkness taunted him, Azol drew strength from his newfound purpose, his love for Aria, and the belief that he could be more than the monster he had been.

In a moment of revelation, Azol harnessed the latent power within him—the power of redemption—and transformed into a being of light and strength, shattering the chains of darkness that had bound him.

With a resounding cry, Azol vanquished the malevolent entity, breaking the cycle of darkness that had plagued him for centuries. The realms rejoiced at the triumph of the demon hero, now reborn as a champion of hope and redemption.

From that day forward, Azol became a legendary figure—a symbol of transformation and the capacity for goodness within even the darkest souls. His tale echoed through the realms, inspiring others to believe in their own potential for change and to find heroism in the unlikeliest of places.

And so, the demon hero, Azol, embraced his newfound identity with courage and humility, proving that even a demon can rise above their past and become a hero of light.

The Babysitter's Whispered Secret

In a peaceful suburban neighborhood, an ominous secret lingered in the shadows—a mysterious murder that had never been solved. The locals spoke of eerie whispers that haunted the night, but the truth remained buried beneath a thick shroud of darkness.

Amidst the community's unease, there was a reliable and responsible teenage babysitter named Emma. She was known for her gentle demeanor and loving care for the children she looked after.

One moonlit evening, Emma was babysitting young Tommy while his parents attended a late-night event. As bedtime approached, she read him a bedtime story, hoping to chase away any lingering fears that the night might bring.

As she tucked Tommy into bed, she noticed a peculiar glimmer in his eyes—a hint of curiosity that prompted her to ask, "Is there something on your mind, Tommy?"

Tommy hesitated, looking around as if he were afraid to speak. With a gentle smile, Emma leaned closer and whispered, "You can tell me anything, I promise."

Encouraged by her words, Tommy finally spoke, "I hear whispers at night. They come from the closet."

Emma's heart skipped a beat, wondering if the whispers were a product of an active imagination or something more sinister. But she knew she couldn't dismiss Tommy's fears, no matter how young he was.

With her babysitter instincts taking over, Emma decided to investigate. She approached the closet and, with a deep breath, swung the door open.

The room was filled with an eerie silence, but Emma thought she could hear a faint whisper too. As she strained her ears, she discovered a hidden compartment within the closet—a dusty old box that seemed out of place.

Her curiosity piqued, Emma reached for the box and carefully opened it. Inside, she found old letters and newspaper clippings, all hinting at the unsolved murder that had haunted the neighborhood.

The chilling truth unraveled before her—the murder had taken place right in Tommy's home many years ago. The whispers that had haunted the child's nights were the echoes of a past tragedy, the restless souls seeking justice.

Determined to uncover the truth, Emma delved deeper into the box and discovered a letter from the murderer, confessing their heinous act. The letter had never been found by the authorities, and the killer had managed to escape justice.

Shaken by the revelation, Emma knew she had to do the right thing. She contacted the police and handed over the evidence that had been hidden for so long.

As the investigation reopened, the whispers in the house seemed to grow louder. But they were no longer filled with fear; they carried a sense of gratitude and relief.

With the truth finally exposed, the neighborhood found closure, and the whispers ceased. The murderer was apprehended, and the souls of the victims found peace.

Emma's bravery and compassion had not only protected Tommy but had also brought justice to a long-forgotten crime.

From that night on, Emma became known as the babysitter who had uncovered the whispered secret—a tale of courage, compassion, and the profound impact that one caring person can have on the lives of those they protect.

Claws of Retribution

In a remote forest, where nature's majesty reigned supreme, there lived a fearsome and powerful bear named Thorin. Once, Thorin had lived peacefully with his family, but that tranquility was shattered when a group of ruthless poachers invaded their territory.

Driven by greed and disregard for nature, the poachers slaughtered Thorin's family, leaving him wounded and grief-stricken. From that moment, revenge burned fiercely in his heart, and he vowed to make the poachers pay for their heinous act.

As the seasons changed, Thorin began plotting his revenge. He watched the poachers from afar, studying their patterns and weaknesses. He knew that retribution required patience and cunning, traits he possessed in abundance.

One moonlit night, when the forest lay shrouded in darkness, Thorin struck. His massive form moved like a shadow, swift and silent. With the element of surprise on his side, he unleashed his fury upon the poachers' camp, catching them off guard.

Fear and chaos erupted as the poachers desperately tried to defend themselves against the vengeful bear. Thorin's claws tore through their defenses, and his roars shook the very ground they stood on.

The poachers had underestimated the bear's intelligence and capacity for vengeance. One by one, they fell, paying the price for the atrocities they had committed.

As the night wore on, the camp fell eerily silent, the poachers defeated and scattered like leaves in the wind. Thorin's revenge had been exacted, but the void left by his family's loss still gnawed at his heart.

In the aftermath of the fierce battle, a young woman named Elara stumbled upon the scene. She had been camping in the forest, drawn by its beauty and serenity.

Instead, she found devastation and a solitary bear standing amidst the wreckage. Contrary to her initial fear, Elara sensed a profound sadness in the bear's eyes—a deep sorrow that mirrored her own losses in life.

Approaching cautiously, Elara extended a hand of empathy to Thorin, who, surprisingly, did not lash out. Instead, he regarded her with a mixture of wariness and curiosity.

Elara understood the pain of loss and the yearning for revenge, and she recognized a kindred spirit in Thorin. As the days passed, she returned to the forest, earning the bear's trust through acts of kindness and understanding.

Through their unique bond, Elara learned of Thorin's tragic past and his desire for revenge. But she also realized that retribution had not brought him the peace he sought.

With time and patience, Elara showed Thorin that revenge did not heal wounds or mend broken hearts. It only perpetuated a cycle of pain and suffering.

Moved by Elara's wisdom and compassion, Thorin began to find solace in her presence. He discovered that revenge was not the path he truly desired—it was healing and redemption.

As the years passed, Elara and Thorin became inseparable. Their friendship bridged the gap between human and bear, showing that understanding and compassion could break the chains of vengeance.

Together, they roamed the forest, spreading a message of coexistence and respect for all creatures. Thorin became a symbol of redemption, a bear who had once sought revenge but had found healing through love and understanding.

And so, the tale of Thorin the vengeful bear transformed into a story of forgiveness and growth, a testament to the transformative power of empathy and the extraordinary bond between a woman and the creature she had helped find a path to redemption.

Battleground of Beasts

In the untamed wilderness, where the mountains stood tall and the moon cast its silver glow, a fierce battle for survival unfolded. Among the ancient trees and rugged terrain, a powerful bear named Kaelen roamed, protecting his territory with unwavering strength.

But in the shadowy depths of the forest, a pack of cunning and relentless wolves lurked—the Bloodfang pack. They had their eyes set on Kaelen's domain, seeking to expand their territory and dominate the land.

As the seasons changed and tensions escalated, the inevitable clash between the bear and the wolves drew near.

One fateful night, under the eerie light of the full moon, the Bloodfang pack struck. Their howls pierced the stillness, warning of the impending attack.

Kaelen, a formidable adversary, faced the onslaught with courage and ferocity. The wolves circled him, their eyes glinting with hunger and determination. But Kaelen would not back down, defending his territory and his life with every ounce of strength he possessed.

With a thunderous roar, Kaelen lunged at the leader of the pack, his powerful claws tearing through the air. The wolves fought fiercely, their teeth and claws clashing with the bear's massive frame.

But as the battle raged on, it became apparent that the wolves were not just fighting for territory—they were fighting for survival. The harsh winters had taken a toll on their food supply, pushing them to the brink of starvation.

In the midst of the chaos, Kaelen sensed their desperation. He saw the hunger in their eyes, and a realization struck him—the wolves were not his enemies; they were simply trying to survive.

A moment of empathy flooded Kaelen's heart. He could easily overpower the wolves, but he chose a different path. In a display of unexpected mercy, he let out a warning roar, urging the wolves to retreat.

As the wolves hesitated, uncertain of the bear's intentions, Kaelen stepped back, granting them an opportunity to escape.

The wolves, sensing the sincerity in the bear's actions, took the chance and disappeared into the night, their tails between their legs. The battle had ended, but not in bloodshed—it had ended in an unexpected act of compassion.

From that night on, a newfound respect permeated the forest. The wolves and the bear found a delicate balance, coexisting and understanding the struggle each species faced to survive in the wilderness.

The tale of Kaelen and the wolves spread far and wide, becoming a legend of unity and compassion—a testament to the power of empathy and the strength in choosing to end a cycle of violence.

And so, in the battleground of beasts, a fierce clash had turned into an unforgettable display of mercy—a story that would echo through the ages as a reminder that even in the wilderness, understanding and empathy could tame the savage heart and forge a path towards harmony.

The Secrets of the Whispering Woods

In a quaint village nestled beside an ancient forest, the Whispering Woods held a chilling secret—a mystery that sent shivers down the spines of all who dared to venture near. Whispers of bodies found deep within the dense foliage spread fear and intrigue among the villagers.

Despite the rumors, a group of curious and adventurous kids—Alex, Emily, and Ben—could not resist the allure of the Whispering Woods. Fuelled by curiosity and a desire for adventure, they decided to uncover the truth behind the haunting tales.

One misty morning, the trio set out on their expedition. The forest was alive with the rustling of leaves, and the air was thick with a sense of foreboding.

As they delved deeper into the woods, they stumbled upon an old and abandoned cabin. Its windows were boarded shut, and the door creaked ominously in the breeze. But something drew them inside, as if an invisible force guided their steps. To their astonishment, they discovered a hidden trapdoor beneath a worn-out rug. With a mix of excitement and trepidation, they pried it open, revealing a hidden chamber below.

The chamber held ancient artifacts, dusty books, and faded maps. As the kids examined the items, they pieced together the chilling truth—the Whispering Woods had once been the hiding place of a notorious group of bandits, who had terrorized the village generations ago.

As they delved deeper into the mysteries of the cabin, they found evidence of the bandits' wrongdoings—the bodies of their victims buried in unmarked graves within the woods.

Horror struck the hearts of the young explorers, but they knew they had to bring the truth to light. Armed with the evidence, they rushed back to the village, determined to uncover the secrets buried in the Whispering Woods.

With the villagers' help, the kids led a daring investigation, unearthing the tragic history of the bandits' reign of terror. Families who had long wondered about the fate of their ancestors finally found closure, and the woods that had once been shrouded in mystery now held a bittersweet tale of the past.

The story of the brave kids and their discovery spread throughout the village, earning them the title of "The Woods' Whisperers."

Their courage and determination had revealed the truth that had haunted their community for generations.

With time, the Whispering Woods lost its ominous aura, and the kids found solace in knowing that the secrets of the past had been laid to rest.

The Whispering Woods became a place of wonder and fascination, a reminder that even in the darkest of places, the curiosity and bravery of children could shine a light on the truth and bring healing to the scars of history. And so, the mystery that had once gripped the village became a tale of resilience, friendship, and the power of discovery.

The Enchanted Forest's Mad Witch

In the heart of an ancient and mystical forest, where the trees whispered ancient secrets and the air was tinged with magic, there lived a mysterious and reclusive figure a mad witch.

The villagers spoke of her with fear and trepidation, claiming she wielded dark and uncontrollable powers. They warned their children never to venture into the depths of the Enchanted Forest, for the mad witch's wrath was said to be swift and merciless.

But amidst the tales of her madness and malevolence, there were whispers of a tragic past that had shaped the witch's destiny. Long ago, she had been a kind and gifted healer, admired and loved by the villagers. However, an unfortunate twist of fate led to the loss of her loved ones, and grief and sorrow consumed her heart.

The once benevolent healer withdrew from the world, seeking solace within the embrace of the Enchanted Forest. There, she communed with the spirits of nature and found refuge in the arms of solitude.

Years passed, and the witch's pain festered, twisting her magic into something dark and unpredictable. The villagers, unable to understand her suffering, branded her as mad and dangerous.

Amidst the rumors and fear, a young girl named Eliza felt a different kind of curiosity. Drawn by the allure of the Enchanted Forest and the mystery of the mad witch, she ventured into the woods, guided by her heart's compassion.

As she neared the witch's secluded dwelling, Eliza sensed an overwhelming sadness emanating from within. Despite the warnings of danger, she pushed forward, determined to understand the truth.

Inside the witch's domain, Eliza found a woman weathered by grief, her eyes haunted by memories. The girl's genuine concern touched a long-forgotten part of the witch's soul.

"Why are you here?" the witch asked, her voice trembling with a mixture of anger and vulnerability.

"I came to understand you," Eliza replied softly. "I believe there's more to your story than what the villagers say."

The witch hesitated, torn between pushing the girl away and finding solace in sharing her burden.

With patient persistence, Eliza sat with the witch and listened as she poured out her heart—a tale of loss, pain, and regret that had trapped her in a cycle of despair.

Eliza's empathy and understanding touched the depths of the witch's soul, stirring feelings she had thought long buried. The young girl's compassion broke through the walls she had built around her heart.

In that moment, the mad witch realized that she didn't need to be defined by the darkness that had consumed her. Eliza's kindness had shown her that there was still hope for healing and redemption. With Eliza's friendship and the solace of the

Enchanted Forest, the witch's heart began to mend. Her magic, once tainted by sorrow, slowly found balance again, restoring harmony to the forest she had once loved. As days turned to weeks, the villagers noticed a change in the Enchanted Forest—the malevolent aura that once surrounded the witch had dissipated. The forest seemed to come alive with newfound magic, its beauty and wonder restored. Word spread of Eliza's friendship with the mad witch, and the villagers' fear began to wane. They realized that there was more to the enigmatic figure than they had once believed. The story of the mad witch and Eliza became a tale of compassion and understanding—a reminder that even in the darkest corners of the heart, the light of friendship and empathy could bring healing and transformation. And so, the Enchanted Forest's mad witch found her path to redemption and a chance to reclaim the beauty of her magic and the love she had once lost.

The Ugly Witch's Quest for True Beauty

In a distant village, there lived an ugly witch named Agatha. With her hunched back and warts, she was shunned and feared by the villagers, who believed her to be wicked and dangerous. But beneath her gnarled exterior, Agatha possessed a heart longing for acceptance and love.

The village was abuzz with excitement as the annual Beauty Festival approached. The celebration honored the most beautiful among them, leaving Agatha feeling even more isolated.

Determined to find a way to be beautiful, Agatha delved into ancient tomes and magical texts, searching for a spell that could transform her appearance. In her research, she stumbled upon a legend of an enchanted mirror hidden deep in the heart of the forest—a mirror that had the power to reveal true beauty.

Fuelled by hope, Agatha set out on her quest. The forest was dense and treacherous, but she pressed on, her heart yearning for the chance to be beautiful and accepted.

As she ventured deeper, she encountered a kind-hearted and wise old midge named Ollie. Despite Agatha's ugly appearance, Ollie saw past the surface and recognized the pain in her eyes.

"Why do you seek beauty, dear witch?" Ollie asked, his voice gentle and soothing.

"I'm tired of being ugly and rejected by the world," Agatha confessed. "I want to be beautiful, so the villagers will accept me."

Ollie pondered her words before speaking again. "True beauty lies not in appearance, but in one's heart and actions. Your quest for acceptance should be about embracing who you are and showing kindness to others."

Agatha considered Ollie's words, realizing the truth in his wisdom. Perhaps her pursuit of beauty had been misguided all along.

Undeterred, they continued their journey together, and at last, they reached the heart of the forest, where the enchanted mirror awaited.

As Agatha gazed into the mirror, she saw not her ugly reflection, but a glimpse of her true self—the kindness, compassion, and bravery that she had never recognized before.

Tears welled up in her eyes as she understood that true beauty was not an external transformation but a discovery of the goodness within.

With newfound clarity, Agatha realized that the villagers' judgment did not define her worth. It was her actions and the love she showed that truly mattered.

Agatha returned to the village, no longer seeking validation from others but carrying the knowledge of her inner beauty.

To her surprise, the villagers were taken aback by her transformation—not the change in her appearance but the change in her heart. As she extended acts of kindness and offered help to those in need, their perception of her shifted.

Agatha's true beauty touched the hearts of the villagers, and slowly, their fear and prejudice faded away. They came to see the kind and compassionate woman she had always been.

The Beauty Festival arrived, and Agatha stood amidst the crowd. Though her appearance remained the same, she felt a newfound sense of confidence and acceptance.

As the festival celebrated beauty, the villagers finally understood the true meaning of the word. They saw beauty in Agatha's actions, in her empathy, and in her brave pursuit of self-acceptance.

And so, the tale of the ugly witch's quest for true beauty became a story of self-discovery and acceptance—a reminder that beauty lies not in appearance but in the heart, and that the quest for acceptance begins with embracing one's true self.

The Witch's Rescue

In a realm where darkness and magic intertwined, a powerful and benevolent witch named Selene lived in a secluded cottage at the edge of a haunted forest. Her knowledge of ancient spells and potions made her revered among the villagers, who sought her aid in times of need.

However, lurking in the shadows was a sinister vampire named Viktor, thirsty for power and craving the witch's magic. He coveted Selene's abilities, believing they would grant him unimaginable strength and dominion over the realm.

One moonless night, while the forest echoed with eerie whispers, Viktor and his minions descended upon the cottage. With a flash of fangs and supernatural speed, they kidnapped Selene, intending to force her to reveal her most guarded secrets.

As dawn broke and the villagers discovered Selene's empty cottage, fear and desperation gripped their hearts. They knew they needed a savior who could face the malevolent vampire and rescue their beloved witch.

Amidst the chaos, a brave and valiant young hunter named Tristan stepped forward. He had grown up hearing stories of Selene's kindness and wisdom and knew he could not stand idly by while she was in peril. Driven by determination, Tristan ventured deep into the haunted forest, where the vampire's lair lay concealed. Armed with enchanted silver weapons, he prepared to face the undead creatures that guarded Selene.

Inside the vampire's lair, Tristan faced countless trials and dangers, but he pressed on, knowing that every moment counted. His heart pounded with fear, but his resolve remained unyielding.

At last, he found Selene held captive in a dimly lit chamber, weakened but still defiant. She warned Tristan of Viktor's treachery and urged him to flee for his safety.

But Tristan refused to abandon her. "I've come to rescue you, Selene," he declared, his voice unwavering. "I won't leave you to face this evil alone."

With newfound strength, Selene cast a powerful spell to weaken the vampire's hold on her. Together, they fought side by side, their determination to defeat Viktor uniting their powers.

The battle was fierce, with claws and spells clashing in the darkness. But in the end, it was Tristan's unyielding courage and Selene's mastery of magic that triumphed over Viktor's malevolence.

As dawn approached, Viktor retreated into the shadows, his thirst for power left unquenched. The haunted forest trembled with relief as the evil presence dispersed.

With Selene rescued and Viktor defeated, the village rejoiced, celebrating Tristan's bravery and Selene's indomitable spirit. The witch and the hunter became heroes, forever etched in the annals of their realm's history.

But the bond forged during their quest ran deeper than gratitude. Tristan and Selene found solace in each other's company, their admiration and respect blossoming into an unexpected friendship, and perhaps something more.

From that day on, the tale of the witch's rescue became a story of courage, unity, and the transformative power of a brave heart. In the face of darkness and danger, two unlikely allies had shown that even the most formidable of foes could be overcome by the strength of love and valor.

Zombies in the Hill

Once upon a time, in a peaceful village nestled at the foot of a mysterious hill, a group of adventurous kids lived—Emma, Liam, and Noah. They were known for their curiosity and fearlessness, always seeking thrilling escapades.

One sunny afternoon, while playing near the hill, the kids noticed strange and eerie noises emanating from its depths. Curiosity piqued, they decided to investigate the source of the mysterious sounds.

As they ventured closer, they discovered an ancient cave hidden among the tall grasses. Hesitant but excited, they entered the dark passage, unaware of the secrets it held.

Inside, they were met with a sight that sent shivers down their spines—zombies! Groaning and shuffling, the undead creatures roamed the cave, their eyes glazed with hunger.

Emma, Liam, and Noah knew they had to act quickly. With courage in their hearts, they devised a plan to outwit the zombies and escape the perilous cave.

Emma, being clever and resourceful, suggested using the shiny marbles they had in their pockets as a distraction. The kids scattered the marbles on the cave floor, causing the zombies to stumble and trip.

As the zombies struggled to regain their balance, Liam, known for his agility, guided the group to climb the rocky walls, staying out of the zombies' reach.

But their adventure had only just begun, for they discovered a mysterious glowing crystal at the cave's heart. It pulsed with an otherworldly energy, hinting at ancient magic.

Noah, the most inquisitive of the trio, couldn't resist the allure of the crystal. Against his friends' warnings, he reached out to touch it.

As Noah's fingers brushed against the crystal's surface, a brilliant light engulfed the cave. The zombies froze in their tracks, seemingly held in place by the enchanting glow.

To their amazement, the crystal's magic had tamed the undead, transforming them into peaceful beings. No longer dangerous, the zombies communicated through soft whispers, grateful to be free from their cursed existence.

Emma, Liam, and Noah listened as the zombies shared their tale—their quest to find the crystal to break the curse that had befallen them. Through the ages, they had been trapped in the hill, unable to escape until someone pure of heart touched the crystal.

United in their mission, the kids and the zombies worked together to uncover the crystal's true purpose. With the combined magic of the crystal and the kids' bravery, the curse was finally broken.

As the sun set over the hill, the zombies bid farewell to their newfound friends, forever free to roam the world without fear. Emma, Liam, and Noah returned to the village, their hearts filled with joy and pride in their courageous adventure.

From that day on, the tale of the brave adventure—where kids and zombies joined forces—became a cherished story in the village. It taught the children the value of bravery, compassion, and the transformative power of friendship.

And so, the village children continued to explore, knowing that even in the darkest of places, true courage and kind hearts could turn a terrifying tale into a heartwarming adventure.

The Haunting of Hollowbrook

In the small town of Hollowbrook, a legend whispered among the children—a chilling tale of zombies that roamed the haunted graveyard at the edge of town. No one dared venture near the eerie place after dark, for fear of awakening the undead.

Among the kids were three curious friends—Lucy, Max, and Jake. Despite the warnings, their fascination with the supernatural led them to the graveyard one moonlit night.

As they tiptoed through the rustling leaves, the graveyard's tombstones loomed like ghostly sentinels. The air felt heavy with the weight of unseen eyes, and the kids couldn't shake the feeling of being watched.

"Are you sure we should be here?" Max whispered, his voice quivering with unease.

"Come on, it's just a spooky story," Lucy reassured, though she couldn't deny the goosebumps on her arms.

They reached the center of the graveyard, where an ancient crypt stood. According to the legend, this was where the zombies were said to rise from their eternal slumber.

Suddenly, the ground beneath them trembled, and eerie moans echoed through the night. Fear clenched at their hearts as the earth seemed to stir.

The friends turned to flee, but it was too late. From the misty ground, the zombies emerged, their eyes empty and hollow, their limbs creaking with each step.

Lucy, Max, and Jake ran for their lives, their screams piercing the silence of the night. The zombies pursued them relentlessly, closing in on their prey.

With no other choice, they sought refuge in the crypt—the very place they had feared the most. The zombies clawed at the door, their bony fingers scraping the wood.

Inside the crypt, Lucy noticed an old book on a dusty pedestal. She quickly opened it, hoping to find a way to escape the relentless zombies.

The book contained an incantation, a spell to send the zombies back to their eternal rest. Lucy read the words aloud, her voice trembling but determined.

As the spell unfolded, a soft glow enveloped the crypt, pushing the zombies back. The ancient magic held them at bay, giving Lucy, Max, and Jake a moment of respite.

Thinking quickly, they each grabbed a vial of sparkling potion from a nearby shelf. The potion was said to repel the undead.

Armed with the vials, they made their move. The friends dashed past the zombies, splashing the potion to keep them at a distance. The creatures recoiled from the potion's power, unable to breach its protective barrier.

Their hearts pounding, they ran until they reached the edge of the graveyard. The spell's magic waned, and the zombies retreated back into the mist, their moans fading into the night.

Breathless but victorious, Lucy, Max, and Jake returned home, knowing they had faced their deepest fears and survived.

From that night on, the legend of the zombies continued to haunt the kids of Hollowbrook, but Lucy, Max, and Jake shared their own story of courage and triumph. They learned that sometimes, facing our fears head-on and relying on the strength of friendship could lead to unexpected bravery and a tale worth sharing with generations to come.

And so, the haunting of Hollowbrook's graveyard became a kids' horror story, reminding them that bravery could conquer even the darkest of legends and that the bonds of friendship could withstand the scariest of nightmares.

The Enchanted Shadows

In a forgotten town hidden amidst ancient woods, a group of adventurous kids—Anna, Tim, and Lily—discovered a mysterious old book in the attic of a long-abandoned house. The book was bound in faded leather and adorned with strange symbols that seemed to shimmer with an eerie glow.

Intrigued by the book's enchanting aura, they flipped through its pages, stumbling upon a spell of dark magic—one that promised to reveal the shadows of the spirit world.

Curiosity getting the better of them, the kids decided to try the spell during a moonlit night, when the veil between worlds was said to be thinnest. With the book open before them, they chanted the incantation, unaware of the ominous forces they were about to unleash.

As the last word left their lips, the room grew cold, and a chilling wind swept through the attic. In an instant, the shadows on the walls began to move, taking on a life of their own.

Out of the darkness emerged a ghostly figure—a spectral apparition clad in tattered garments. The kids gasped, their hearts pounding with fear and awe.

The ghost spoke in a hushed whisper, its voice echoing with sorrow and longing. "You have awakened me from my slumber. Why have you called upon the shadows of the spirit realm?"

Before they could respond, the ghostly figure reached out, its icy fingers grazing their hands. An overwhelming surge of fear washed over them, and they realized the consequences of their impulsive actions.

"We didn't mean to disturb you," Anna stammered. "We were just curious about the spell."

The ghost regarded them with somber eyes. "Curiosity can lead to unexpected consequences," it warned. "Now, the shadows have been unleashed, and they hunger for the living."

As the ghost faded back into the shadows, the room grew darker, and strange shapes moved in the corners. The children's hearts pounded with terror as the shadows seemingly came alive, dancing in macabre patterns.

"We need to find a way to undo the spell," Tim said, his voice trembling.

The kids searched the book for a counter-spell, but to their dismay, it was nowhere to be found. It seemed the magic was irreversible.

With the shadows closing in around them, they realized they had to confront their fears and find a way to appease the restless spirits.

Bravely, they reached out to the ghost, acknowledging their mistake and asking for forgiveness. They promised to find a way to restore the balance between the worlds.

he ghost's expression softened, and a glimmer of understanding shone in its eyes. "You show remorse and courage," it said. "There may still be hope for redemption."

With newfound determination, the kids devised a plan to contain the shadows. They created a magical circle and chanted a binding spell to seal the spirits within the attic.

As the incantation reached its crescendo, the shadows slowly retreated, their malevolent presence dissipating.

Exhausted but triumphant, the kids knew they had learned a valuable lesson—that magic should be treated with respect and caution, for its consequences could be dire.

They returned the book to its rightful place, vowing never to delve into dark magic again. The attic remained a haunted place, but the shadows were contained, and the spirits found a semblance of peace.

From that night on, the kids shared a bond forged through their harrowing encounter with the spirit world. They knew they had faced true horror and lived to tell the tale.

And so, the tale of the Enchanted Shadows became a chilling kids' horror story, reminding them that even the allure of magic had its price and that true bravery lay in acknowledging one's mistakes and facing the shadows that lurked within.

The Mystery of the Kidnapped Ghost

In the heart of a dense and enchanted forest, a group of adventurous kids—Emma, Alex, and Mia—gathered around a crackling campfire one moonlit night. As the flames danced and the stars sparkled above, they decided to share spooky tales to add an extra thrill to their camping adventure.

Mia, the bravest of the trio, decided to tell a tale she had heard from her older brother—the legend of the Kidnapped Ghost.

Long ago, in a village not far from their camping spot, there lived a gentle ghost named Casper. Casper was loved by the villagers, as he brought luck and joy wherever he roamed.

But one fateful night, a group of mischievous spirits from the Spirit Realm decided to play a wicked prank on Casper. They kidnapped him and brought him to their ethereal domain, where time flowed differently from the human world.

Back in the village, days turned into weeks, and Casper's absence cast a shadow of sadness upon the villagers. They missed the ghost's friendly presence and wondered where he had vanished.

Unknown to the villagers, Casper's spirit remained trapped in the Spirit Realm, unable to find a way back to the village. The other spirits played tricks on him, making it even harder for him to return.

In the village, a brave trio of kids—Lucas, Lily, and Owen—heard whispers of the kidnapped ghost. Determined to solve the mystery and rescue their beloved friend, they ventured into the haunted forest, following an ancient map rumored to lead to the Spirit Realm.

As they delved deeper into the forest, they encountered eerie sights and strange sounds. The trees seemed to whisper warnings, and the wind carried ghostly echoes.

Finally, they reached a hidden portal—the gateway to the Spirit Realm. Though fearful, they knew they had to be brave for their friend.

With a deep breath, they stepped through the portal and found themselves in a realm of ethereal beauty and shifting landscapes.

Guided by their unwavering friendship, the kids navigated the Spirit Realm, facing riddles and challenges set by the mischievous spirits. At every turn, they showcased courage and compassion, proving themselves worthy of helping Casper.

At last, they found Casper trapped in a maze of mirrors that distorted his reflection. With a glimmer of hope in his eyes, he reached out to them.

"Dare you to break the mirrors," a spirit challenged, its voice echoing through the realm.

Ignoring their fear, the kids grabbed their campfire mirrors and shattered them one by one. The shards dispersed like shimmering stars, freeing Casper from his ethereal prison.

The Spirit Realm trembled as the mirrors shattered, and the mischievous spirits cowered. With Casper's guidance, the kids returned to the human world, carrying the kidnapped ghost safely back to the village.

The village rejoiced, and the kids were hailed as heroes. Casper's joyous laughter once again filled the air, and the villagers thanked the trio for their courage and friendship.

From that night on, the tale of the Kidnapped Ghost became a cherished campfire story among the kids. It taught them the power of bravery, compassion, and the strength of friendship—together, they had ventured into the unknown and brought back the light that had been stolen from their beloved ghostly friend.

And so, the mystery of the Kidnapped Ghost lived on, a heartwarming tale of adventure and the triumph of friendship, to be shared with generations of young campfire storytellers.

The Bewitched Woods

Deep within the heart of a mystical forest stood a place known as the Bewitched Woods—a realm of ancient trees and whispered enchantments. It was a forest where magic roamed free, and legends of eerie creatures haunted the imagination of the local children.

Among the kids who dared to venture near the Bewitched Woods were Sophie, Jack, and Lily. One chilly evening, as the sun dipped below the horizon, they decided to explore the forest to uncover its mysteries.

As they stepped into the enchanted woodland, the air turned cold, and the trees seemed to sway with an otherworldly rhythm. Yet, undeterred, they pressed on, determined to unravel the secrets hidden in the shadows.

As they wandered deeper into the woods, strange things began to happen. The trees seemed to come alive, their branches reaching out like ghostly hands. The kids felt as though they were being watched by unseen eyes.

Jack's heart raced, but he tried to sound brave. "There's nothing to be afraid of. It's just a spooky forest."

But as they continued, they stumbled upon a clearing, where a peculiar stone altar stood. A single beam of moonlight illuminated the ancient stone, revealing peculiar symbols etched into its surface.

Sophie, with her insatiable curiosity, traced her finger along the markings, unknowingly triggering an ancient spell.

In an instant, the forest transformed—the trees twisted and contorted, forming eerie shapes. The ground trembled, and from the shadows emerged a host of ghastly creatures.

Glowing eyes peered from the darkness, and eerie whispers filled the air. The kids' hearts pounded with terror as they found themselves surrounded by the forest's malevolent enchantments.

Lily, the most imaginative of the trio, spoke in a trembling voice, "We need to find a way to break the spell and escape this haunted place."

Their only chance of survival lay in undoing the enchantment that Sophie had inadvertently triggered.

With quick thinking, they recalled a legend—the ancient Forest Guardian, who held the power to lift curses from the forest.

They retraced their steps, following an ancient path known only to the wisest of forest-dwellers. The trail led to an ancient tree, its trunk adorned with mystical symbols.

Whispers of the forest guardian echoed in their minds, guiding them to perform a ritual of courage and unity. Together, they chanted ancient verses and held hands, their bond strengthening with each word.

The forest trembled, and the ghastly creatures vanished into the shadows. The enchantment that had shrouded the woods began to wane.

As the last verse echoed through the woods, the forest guardian appeared—a majestic, ethereal figure with shimmering wings and a kind smile.

"You have shown bravery and friendship," the guardian said, "and so, the Bewitched Woods shall be enchanted no more."

With the spell broken, the forest returned to its peaceful state—the trees no longer twisted, and the eerie creatures disappeared.

The kids returned to their village, forever changed by their encounter in the Bewitched Woods. They now knew the true value of courage, friendship, and the power of the imagination. From that night on, the tale of the Bewitched Woods became a kids' horror story, one that reminded them to be wary of ancient enchantments and to cherish the strength that came from facing their fears together. And so, the legend of the Bewitched Woods lived on, a chilling but empowering tale to be told around campfires, teaching the young ones that sometimes, the most magical adventures could be found in the darkest of places.

The Haunting of Moonlight Forest

In the heart of Moonlight Forest, where the moon's silvery glow bathed the ancient trees, a chilling mystery was said to lurk—a legend of a fearsome creature that emerged under the full moon—the dreaded Werewolf.

Among the kids who heard the spine-chilling tales were Anna, Ben, and Emily. One moonlit night, they dared each other to venture into Moonlight Forest to uncover the truth behind the eerie legends.

As they tiptoed through the whispering trees, the forest seemed to come alive with hidden eyes watching their every move. Goosebumps rose on their skin, but they were determined to solve the mystery that had gripped their imaginations.

Unbeknownst to them, the forest was rumored to be a werewolf's territory, and each full moon, the creature would emerge to haunt those who dared to trespass.

As the moon climbed higher in the sky, casting eerie shadows among the trees, the kids heard a haunting howl. Fear clenched at their hearts, but curiosity urged them deeper into the forest.

Following a faint trail, they stumbled upon a secluded glade where the moonlight fell in a silvery pool. The glade was encircled by ancient stones, hinting at the forest's ancient magic.

In the center of the glade stood a mysterious figure—a man with wild eyes and shaggy hair, transforming into a fearsome beast as the moonlight engulfed him.

"It's the werewolf!" Emily gasped, her voice barely a whisper.

so the transformation completed, the werewolf turned its gaze toward the children. But instead of charging at them, it seemed to hesitate, its eyes flickering with recognition.

Anna, with her compassionate heart, stepped forward. "Who are you?" she asked bravely.

The werewolf's growl softened, and a hint of humanity returned to its eyes. "I was once a man named Evan," it said, its voice tinged with sadness. "Cursed by an ancient spell, I transform into a werewolf under the full moon."

"Is there a way to break the curse?" Ben inquired, trying to hide his fear.

Evan nodded, revealing that a silver amulet hidden in the heart of the forest could lift the curse. But it was heavily guarded by the forest's ancient spirits, and only a true-hearted soul could retrieve it.

Determined to help Evan, the kids agreed to embark on a perilous quest to find the amulet and break the curse. Through moonlit nights and dark shadows, they faced treacherous challenges. They encountered ghostly apparitions and bewitching riddles, but their bond of friendship and bravery carried them forward.

At last, they reached the heart of the forest—a hidden cave where the amulet was said to rest. A guardian spirit stood before them, testing their resolve.

With courage in their hearts, they proved their worthiness to the spirit, earning the right to claim the amulet.

Returning to the glade, they placed the amulet around Evan's neck. A dazzling light surrounded him, and as the moonlight bathed the glade, Evan transformed back into a human. Gratitude filled Evan's eyes as he looked at the kids. "Thank you for breaking the curse and showing me kindness," he said. As the first rays of dawn touched the horizon, the kids bid farewell to Evan, knowing they had not only solved a mystery but also helped a soul find peace. From that night on, the tale of the Haunting of Moonlight Forest became a legendary kids' horror story, a reminder that bravery, friendship, and compassion could conquer even the most terrifying of legends. And so, the moonlit glade in Moonlight Forest held the memory of a transformative adventure, where children faced their fears and discovered the true power of their hearts under the watchful eye of the silver moon.

The Midnight Menace

In the heart of the woods, where moonlight barely pierced the dense canopy, a group of kids huddled around a crackling campfire. The night was filled with spooky tales, but none could match the chilling legend of the Crazy Clown—a haunting figure said to roam the woods at midnight.

Among the kids were Sam, Mia, and Lucas. They listened wide-eyed as the older campers weaved tales of the crazy clown's antics and mischievous pranks.

As the campfire flames danced, casting eerie shadows on the trees, the older kids finally decided to share the story of their encounter with the infamous Crazy Clown.

Years ago, a group of campers had arrived at this very spot, unaware of the clown's malevolence. They had laughed and played, not heeding the warnings of the locals.

But as the clock struck midnight, the atmosphere changed—a haunting laughter echoed through the woods. The campers froze in fear as the Crazy Clown emerged from the shadows, its face painted with a sinister grin.

The clown's eyes glowed with a malevolent gleam, and its cackles sent shivers down their spines. The woods seemed to close in around them, trapping them in its horrifying embrace.

Terrified, the campers fled in all directions, trying to escape the clown's menacing grip. But the clown was relentless, always one step behind, appearing and disappearing in the darkness.

As the campers raced through the woods, they stumbled upon an old abandoned cabin—the clown's lair. Desperation pushed them inside, hoping to find refuge.

Inside, the cabin was filled with eerie relics—a rusty music box playing a haunting tune, a collection of weathered masks hanging on the walls.

Suddenly, the door slammed shut, and the campers found themselves trapped with the Crazy Clown. Its laughter reverberated through the cabin, and their fears intensified.

But just as the clown's antics seemed to escalate, a brave camper named Josh stood his ground. He confronted the clown, demanding to know why it haunted the woods.

The clown's laughter softened, and a haunting melody filled the air. The music box played a sad tune, revealing the clown's tragic past.

Long ago, the clown had been an entertainer who brought joy to children. But one fateful night, an accident during a performance had left him scarred and disfigured, driving him to madness.

Touched by the clown's sorrowful past, Josh approached him with compassion. "You don't have to be a monster. You can find redemption," he said.

The campers joined in, offering friendship and understanding. They urged the clown to let go of his anger and embrace the memory of the laughter he once brought.

Moved by their kindness, the Crazy Clown's demeanor softened, and the malevolent glint in its eyes faded.

With a final laugh, the clown vanished into the night, leaving the campers to breathe a sigh of relief.

From that night on, the legend of the Crazy Clown lived on, a cautionary tale told around campfires, reminding kids of the power of compassion and the potential for redemption.

And so, the Midnight Menace became a haunting campfire story, one that taught the young campers that even in the darkest of nights, a spark of kindness could bring light to the most terrifying of encounters.